the jolly bar

By Annie North Bedford
Illustrated by Tibor Gergely

🦋 A GOLDEN BOOK • NEW YORK

Copyright © 1950, renewed 1978 by Random House, Inc. All rights reserved under International and Pan-American Copyright Conventions. Published in the United States by Golden Books, an imprint of Random House Children's Books, a division of Random House, Inc., New York, and simultaneously in Canada by Random House of Canada Limited, Toronto. Originally published in 1950 in slightly different form by Simon & Schuster, Inc., and Artists and Writers Guild, Inc. Golden Books, A Golden Book, A Little Golden Book, the G colophon, and the distinctive gold spine are registered trademarks of Random House, Inc. A Little Golden Book Classic is a trademark of Random House, Inc. Library of Congress Control Number: 2003105968 ISBN: 0-375-82842-7 www.goldenbooks.com Printed in the United States of America   First Random House Edition 2004 1 0 9 8 7 6 5

Said Farmer Brown, "Tra-la, tra-lee!
Today is my birthday, lucky me!
I'll give my animals a treat—
for each, what he likes best to eat."

First he took a pan of oats, of course,
to the baby colt and the mother horse.

For the cow and calf he set corn down.
"'Cause today is my birthday," said Farmer Brown.

The big white ram and the fat black sheep
ate all the grain in a great big heap.

The gobbling turkey ate and ate until
he had to admit he'd eaten his fill.

The chickens and rooster got their food—
enough for all their hungry brood.

And so did the duck, and so did the drake
and the ducklings down beside the lake.

The dog got bones to bury and to chew.

The cat got milk—and the kitten did, too.

When all the animals had been fed,
Farmer Brown left, and the spotted cow said:

"Kind Farmer Brown! What would you say
we could do for him on his birthday?"

"We'll pull his loads smoothly, with never a jolt,"
said the big brown horse and her little brown colt.

"Moo-oo, I'll give him lots of milk," said the cow.
Said her calf, "I will, too, someday, somehow!"

"Baa-aa, we'll give him wool," said the sheep.
"For our fleece is soft and warm and deep."

"Gobble!" said the turkey. "As well as I am able,
I'll decorate his Thanksgiving table."

"Cluck! I will give him eggs," said the hen.
Said the rooster, "I'll wake him in the
mornings, then."

"Quack! He can have duck eggs," said the duck.
"And I'll swim on his pond," said the drake,
"for luck."

"Bow-wow!" said the dog. "I'll guard his house both night and day, but most of all when he's away!"

"Mew! We'll catch his mice," said the cat.
"We're good hunters," said the kitten.
"Farmer Brown will tell you that."

Inside the farmhouse was another treat—
a beautiful birthday cake to eat.
What a happy birthday for Farmer Brown!